HOW'S YOUR HEALTH?

Allergies

Angela Royston

A+

Smart Apple Media

Smart Apple Media is published by Black Rabbit Books
P.O. Box 3263, Mankato, Minnesota 56002

Printed in the United States

Published by arrangement with the Watts Publishing Group Ltd, London.

Editor: Sarah Eason
Design: Paul Myerscough
Illustration: Annie Boberg and Geoff Ward
Picture research: Sarah Jameson
Consultant: Dr. Stephen Earwicker

Acknowledgements:
The publisher would like to thank the following for permission to reproduce photographs: Alamy p.14, p.22, p.23, p.25, p.27; Istockphoto p.8; Corbis p.15; OSF p.24; Getty p.6; Tudor Photography p.7, p.10, p.12, p.21; Chris Fairclough Photography p.9, p.11, p.16, p.17, p.18, p.20, p.26.

Library of Congress Cataloging-in-Publication Data

Royston, Angela.
    Allergies / Angela Royston.
    p. cm.—(Smart Apple Media. How's your health?)
    Includes index.
    Summary: "Describes the symptoms and treatment of food allergies, skin allergies, and breathing allergies"—Provided by publisher.
    ISBN 978-1-59920-220-4
    1. Allergy—Juvenile literature. I. Title.
RC585.R69 2009
616.97—dc22   2007035174

9 8 7 6 5 4 3 2 1

Contents

What Is an Allergy?

An allergy makes your body react to something as if it is harmful, although it is not harmful to most people.

People can be allergic to different things. Some people are **allergic** to certain foods, such as strawberries or peanuts. These are healthy foods that most people enjoy, but people who are allergic to them will get sick if they eat them.

Some people are allergic to things they touch.
Other people are allergic to things they breathe
in, such as **pollen**. Pollen is a fine dust that is
made in spring and summer by grass, trees, and
flowers. People with **hay fever** are allergic to pollen.
Hay fever makes your eyes sore and your nose run.

Who Has Allergies?

Anyone can have an allergy, but allergies usually run in families. You cannot catch an allergy.

People are more likely to have an allergy if one of their parents is allergic to something. This does not always mean that they will be allergic to the same thing. One of these girls is allergic to chocolate, but her mother is allergic to pollen.

Most of the time, most people with an allergy live like everyone else.

How You Can Help

+ If you have an allergy, stay away from the thing you are allergic to.
+ If someone else has an allergy, keep them away from anything that gives them an allergic reaction.

9

What Is a Food Allergy?

People with food allergies will get sick if they eat the food that they are allergic to.

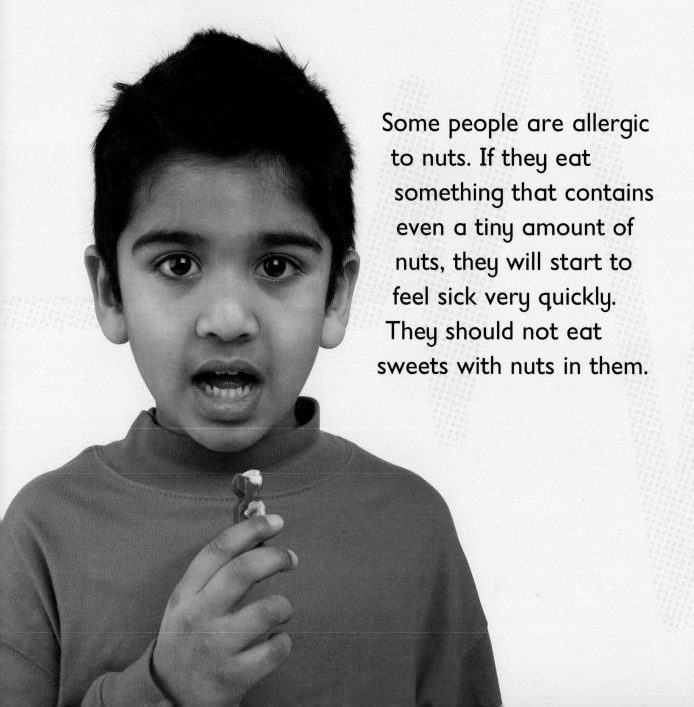

Some people are allergic to nuts. If they eat something that contains even a tiny amount of nuts, they will start to feel sick very quickly. They should not eat sweets with nuts in them.

Foods that May Cause Allergic Reactions

+ Peanuts and other kinds of nuts
+ Eggs
+ Milk, cheese, yogurt, and other foods made from milk
+ **Seafood**, such as shrimp, prawns, and mussels
+ **Soybeans**
+ Things made from **wheat**, such as bread, pasta, cereal, and cookies

People with a nut allergy may get very sick if they eat nuts. They will continue to feel sick until their body has gotten rid of all the nuts they have eaten.

How Do Food Allergies Affect People?

A food allergy can affect someone's mouth, stomach, **intestines**, and skin.

If you eat something you are allergic to, your mouth and throat may swell up and become **numb**. You may get sick and have **diarrhea**.

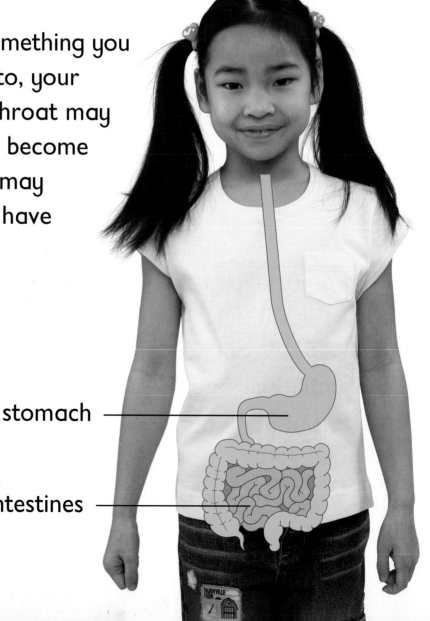

stomach ————

intestines ————

A food allergy can also affect other parts of the body. Your skin may turn red and become itchy. Your nose may run and you may sneeze a lot. You may also feel dizzy.

How You Can Help

+ If the allergy does not make you too sick, rest until you feel better.
+ Keep calm.
+ If someone else is affected by a food allergy, keep them calm.
+ If the person is very sick, ask an adult to call an ambulance right away.

What Is a Breathing Allergy?

A breathing allergy makes you sneeze and your nose run. It is like having a cold.

People who have a breathing allergy are allergic to something they breathe in, such as cigarette smoke. It can affect their lungs and eyes, as well as their nose. They may cough and their eyes may become itchy and swollen.

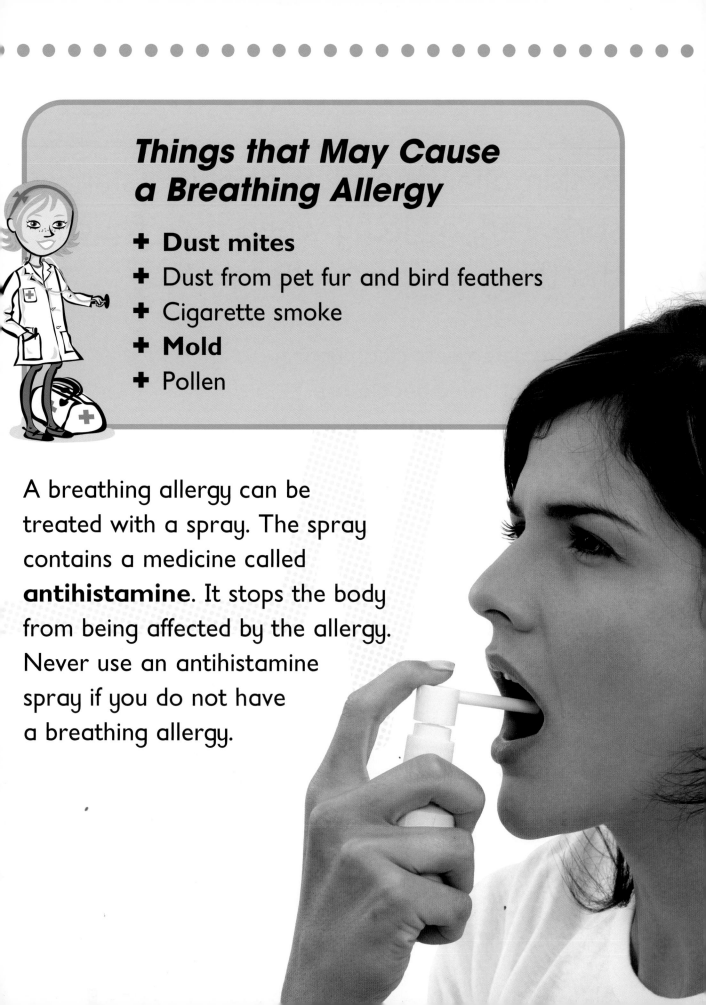

Things that May Cause a Breathing Allergy

+ **Dust mites**
+ Dust from pet fur and bird feathers
+ Cigarette smoke
+ **Mold**
+ Pollen

A breathing allergy can be treated with a spray. The spray contains a medicine called **antihistamine**. It stops the body from being affected by the allergy. Never use an antihistamine spray if you do not have a breathing allergy.

What Is a Skin Allergy?

A skin allergy makes people's skin sore, red, or itchy when they touch the thing they are allergic to.

Laundry detergents clean your clothes, but some people are allergic to the **chemicals** in them. Some people are allergic to detergents with dyes and perfumes.

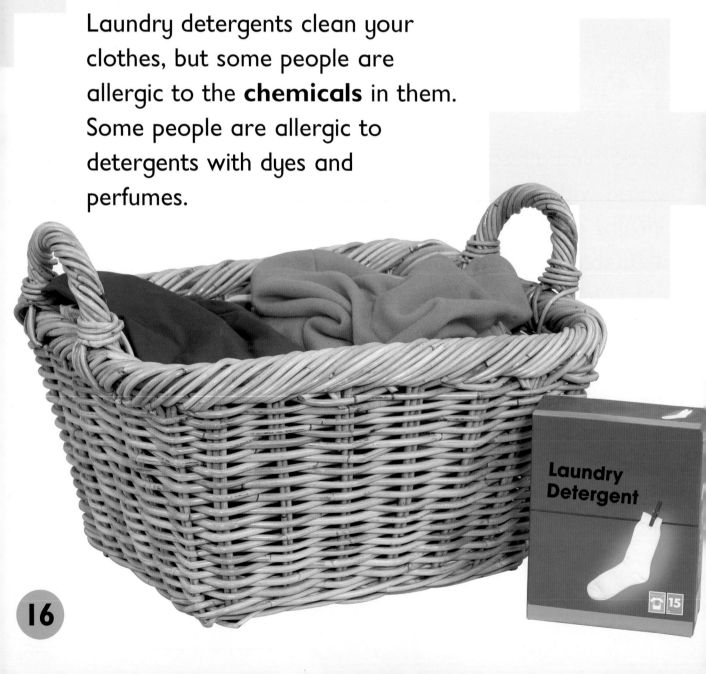

Laundry Detergent

If you have a skin allergy, don't scratch the itch—this will only make it worse. People with **eczema** have patches of very dry, itchy skin. Eczema is often made worse by skin and food allergies.

a skin allergy

Things that Often Cause Skin Allergies

+ Insect bites
+ **Cosmetics**
+ Scented soaps
+ Laundry detergents
+ Household products, such as floor cleaners and bath cleaners

How Are Skin Allergies Treated?

Special creams help soothe skin allergies and stop them from itching.

Different creams can help stop skin from itching and feeling sore. They do not stop the allergy itself, but they can make your skin feel better.

The best way for people to treat a skin allergy is to stay away from the things that they are allergic to. People with skin allergies can buy laundry detergent without dyes and perfumes, pure soap, and cosmetics that do not affect their skin.

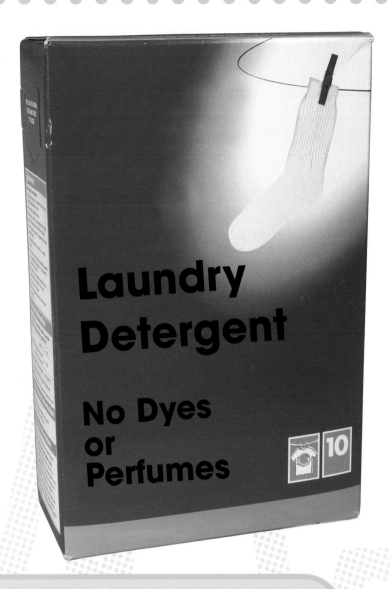

Laundry Detergent

No Dyes or Perfumes

How You Can Help

+ Use a cream as soon as your skin becomes sore or itchy.
+ Don't use cosmetics or laundry detergents that affect your skin.
+ Stay away from things you are allergic to.

What is extreme shock?

Extreme shock is when a person's whole body suddenly reacts very badly to something.

A wasp sting hurts most people and makes a small red mark on their skin. A wasp sting can also cause extreme shock in some people if they are allergic to it. Other things, such as seafood and medicine, can also cause extreme shock.

Symptoms of Extreme Shock

+ **Wheezing** or difficulty breathing
+ Coughing
+ Sickness, diarrhea, and stomachache
+ Heart beating much faster than usual
+ Skin turning red or blue
+ Not being able to think or talk clearly
+ Fainting

Find out what to do if someone has
extreme shock on page 22.

When people suffer from
extreme shock, they may find it
difficult to breathe. They may also
have a stomachache and get sick.
They are affected almost right away.

How Is Extreme Shock Treated?

If you have extreme shock, you must take special medicine right away.

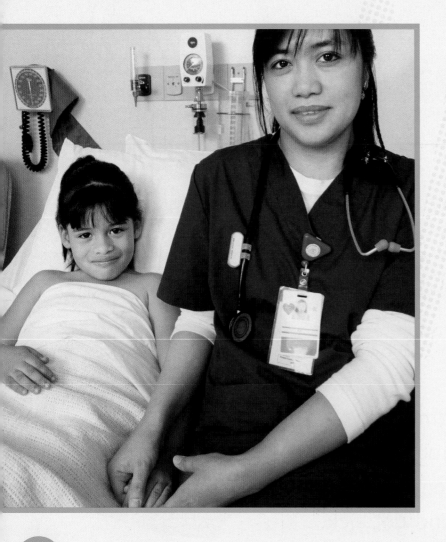

If you suffer from extreme shock, you need to be treated by a doctor very quickly. Call an ambulance right away.

Two medicines are used to treat extreme shock. One is **injected** to help the heart to beat normally. The second medicine is an antihistamine tablet, which people chew to stop their body from reacting badly to the allergy.

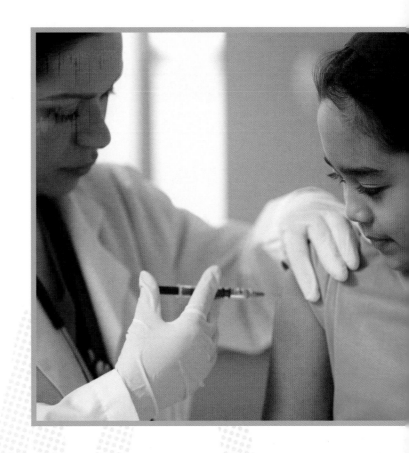

Take Care!

Extreme shock medicines are very strong and must *never* be taken by anyone else. People who know they can suffer from extreme shock should carry their medicine with them. They should also wear a necklace or bracelet that will tell doctors about their allergy.

Is there a Test for Allergies?

Hospitals can test people to see what they are allergic to.

Sometimes people do not know what they are allergic to. In an allergy **clinic**, a nurse puts a small amount of different things a person might be allergic to into their skin.

If someone is allergic to something in the allergy test, it will make their skin turn red.

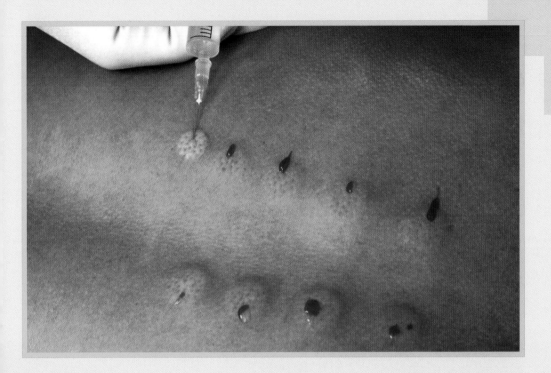

Some allergies can be shown by a **blood test**.

Other Tests

Another way people can find out what they are allergic to is by staying away from all the things that might be causing their allergy. When they start to use each of these things again, one at a time, they should be able to tell which one causes the allergy.

Do Allergies Get Better?

Many children have allergies that get better as they grow older.

Children often grow out of allergies.
This boy is allergic to cats. Many children are allergic to certain foods, such as cheese.

By the time people become adults, they may no longer be allergic. This woman was allergic to pet hair when she was a child. Now she is an adult, and she is no longer allergic. However, many older people become allergic to things that did not affect them before.

Glossary

allergic   to have an allergy.

antihistamine   medicine that stops the body from reacting to something it is allergic to.

blood test   when a small amount of blood is taken from people to find out things about their body.

chemical   powerful substance found in many man-made things, including cleaning supplies and beauty products.

clinic   place where people are treated by doctors and nurses.

cosmetics   creams and makeup that people put on their skin.

diarrhea   when the solid waste your body makes is loose and runny.

dust mite   tiny spider-like animal that lives in house dust.

eczema   condition that makes the skin dry and itchy.

hay fever   allergy to pollen.

inject   the way liquid medicine is put into the body through a needle.

intestine   part of the body that deals with food and waste.

mold   furry coat that grows on old food or damp things.

numb   without feeling.

pollen   fine yellow dust made by flowers, grass, and some trees in spring and early summer.

seafood   sea animals that can be eaten, such as prawns, shrimps and mussels.

soybean   bean that can be made into different foods, such as milk and yogurt.

wheat crop that is made into food, such as bread, cereal, and cookies.

wheeze sound people make when they are having a hard time breathing.

Find Out More

Allergy ABCs—Allergy Info for Kids
www.allergyabcs.com/allergies.htm

Food Allergy News for Kids
www.fankids.org

For Kids: Learning about Allergies
www.kidshealth.org/kid/asthma_basics/related/allergies.html

Every effort has been made by the publisher to ensure that these Web sites contain no inappropriate or offensive material. However, because of the nature of the Internet, it is impossible to guarantee that the contents of these sites will not be altered. We strongly advise that Internet access is supervised by a responsible adult.

Index